The Music Box Murders

The Lizzie Borden Story

Ronda L. Caudill, Ph.D.

Published by Full Moon Publishing, LLC

Glade Spring, VA

ISBN-13: 978-0615998862

ISBN-10: 0615998860

DEDICATION

To my wonderful family who always supports me and provides great inspiration.

CONTENTS

ACKNOWLEDGMENTS

A special thank goes out to Michelle Cornwell-Jordan who published this in her anthology *Lyrical Muse*. I would also like to send out a special thanks to CP Bialois and Jamie White for their awesome editing kills.

CHAPTER 1

It was August 4, 1892 in Fall River, Massachusetts. Abby Borden was in an upstairs bedroom cleaning when she heard a sound behind her. Just as she started to turn her head, someone attacked from behind. The sharp hatchet blade came down hard and repeatedly. Thirteen strikes to the head; blood splattering with each blow. Five strikes missed Abby's head and landed in her torso. Abby never knew it was her own stepdaughter, Lizzie, who had been the savage murderer.

Lizzie turned and sat on the beautiful gold settee with the bloody hatchet in her hands. Laying beside her, her music box played its fateful song. There she sat and waited patiently on her father, Andrew, to return home. She heard the front door open and close. She tip-toed to the top of the stairs to catch a quick glimpse of Andrew hanging his hat on the hat rack beside the front door. Lizzie slipped back into the bedroom where her stepmother lay in a pool of red velvet liquid, already beginning to coagulate.

Lizzie knew her father's morning routine. Andrew Borden would have breakfast, go to the bank to check on his funds and transactions and pick up yesterday's paper, before returning home to it. After finishing the paper, Andrew would then lay back on the couch in the parlor and take a nap.

Knowing how long Andrew's routine took, Lizzie knew the precise moment when he would be in a sound sleep. When the time had come, she calmly closed her music box and put it back into her pocket and stood. Carrying the bloodied hatchet in one hand, Lizzie quietly made her way down the stairs, only creaking one step. She wanted to make certain that he never knew what hit him. As Lizzie approached, she raised the red spattered hatchet above her head, preparing for the ultimate revenge. She relished in that moment.

The hatchet came down hard, splitting Andrew's head and

killing him with the first blow. She struck ten more times, once severing his eyeball in half. Again, blood covered the surrounding area in splashes of crimson. Lizzie leaned over and kissed her father on the forehead. "Now, father, I love you once again. You have paid for your crime."

CHAPTER 2

The year was 1890 and Lizzie Borden was an attractive, single, thirty-year-old woman. Even though she was considered a spinster or an old maid by the standards then, her sister, Emma, was a bit older. It was by choice that the two girls had never married. They were both quite content living at home and to date; no man had swept either off their feet. That was soon to change.

One spring morning, Lizzie was in the garden with the Borden maid, Bridget Sullivan. Lizzie and Emma called her by her name. However, Abby and Andrew Borden never bothered to learn her name; they simply called her by the name of the previous maid, Maggie. Lizzie, Emma, and Bridget prided themselves on the loveliest flower garden in Fall River. They spent many hours grooming and cultivating their little slice of heaven. The Two women had only been in the garden for a short while when they heard someone whistling *Fur Elise*. It was

Lizzie's favorite song. She looked up to see a very attractive

stranger. When their eyes met he had to stop to introduce

himself.

"Hello, ladies. I don't mean to interrupt you, but I must say

this is by far the most beautiful flower garden I have ever seen

in my life. And the gardeners are every bit as beautiful as the

flowers they tend." He reached up, took off his hat, and bowed

to the women. "My name is John Goodman."

Blushing, Lizzie stood to introduce and dust herself off.

Lizzie's curtseyed like a lady should. Bridget curtseyed and

bowed her head, but never said a word. Poor Bridget knew her

place even though the Borden sisters considered her a friend.

"Well, Miss. Borden, I just moved here from Boston. I

bought the old Templeton House around the corner. Maybe I

will see you again soon, since we appear to be neighbors."

"Perhaps," Lizzie said with the slightest smile. She had

never before been interested in a man, but this John Goodman

made her heart skip a beat. John resumed his whistling and

walked away, the sound of that beautiful melody grew fainter

and fainter until it was no more.

Little did Lizzie know; that she and her new friend were

being watched. Andrew stood in the parlor, peering out the

window at the interactions between Lizzie and the stranger.

Andrew waited on Lizzie to come in for lunch before saying

anything about the stranger. He was a very private man and did

not air his dirty laundry for the community to see.

"Lizzie," Andrew said with a stern voice. "Who was that

man and what were you two talking about?" His eyes glared in a

way that had always frightened her.

Lizzie trembled slightly and approached him with great

trepidation. "His name is John Goodman and he just bought the

Templeton House. He was just introducing himself and

complementing the garden. That's all," Lizzie said, bowing her

head slightly and picking at her gardening gloves.

6

Bridget had been right behind Lizzie when Andrew began his questioning. She could see that Lizzie was uncomfortable with Andrew's questioning. Even though Bridget and Lizzie were close, she dared not speak up in Lizzie's defense. She stood with her head bowed, waiting on the questioning to end.

Andrew remained silent as his stern presence intimidated both Lizzie and Bridget. After an eternal pause, Andrew finally spoke, "Don't encourage that man. I don't need him coming around. We are all happy just the way things are around here. You know how I loathe outsiders."

"Yes, Father. I understand," Lizzie replied with her eyes downcast. However her appearance, her heart sung a different tune, a melody she could not deny. She was immediately taken by this man. Lizzie hoped that she would soon be seeing him again. She wasn't prepared to deal with her father's opposition, but she knew there was something about John that made facing the consequences with her father worth it.

"Fine. Now off with you both. Prepare lunch. I am tired of

waiting," Andrew said as he turned and walked off heavy-footed.

Lizzie let out her breath. She didn't realize she had been holding it with the exception of her responding to her father. She and Bridget hurried out of the room and into the kitchen, giggling when they were out of the hearing range of Andrew. They talked in low voices about how attractive John was. They discussed his manners and how debonair he had been. The two girls jumped and turned when they heard the door slam from behind them. Lizzie knew that Andrew would go into an uncontrollable rage at hearing the girls' conversation.

"Oh, Emma. Thank God it's you!" Lizzie said, exhaling.

"I'm happy that it pleases you to have my company," Emma said, wondering what the two girls were up to.

"I thought it was Father," Lizzie said.

"So what is it you are hiding from Father? Whatever it is, you know you shouldn't," Emma said, leaning in close.

"Today the most wonderful thing happened. I met a man. A wonderful handsome, gentle man," Lizzie said.

"You should be careful. If Father finds out..." Emma trailed off.

Lizzie didn't wait for Emma to finish her sentence, "Father knows. That's why I was relieved to see that it was you coming in."

"Oh no, what did he say?" Emma asked.

"He wasn't happy." Lizzie explained how Andrew had seen the interactions between her and John and how he had questioned her about the encounter.

"Lizzie, you should be very careful. You are not planning on pursuing a friendship with this man, are you? Father will definitely not be happy about that. And you will have Abby to deal with as well," Emma said, her eyes alight with warning.

"I know," Lizzie said with a sigh. But she could not shake

the thought of the wonderful stranger she had met less than an hour before.

The three girls finished preparing lunch and Bridget called for Andrew and Abby to come to the dining room. Bridget served everyone and returned to the kitchen to have her meal. It pleased her not to sit in and have a meal with the Borden's. Anytime they were all together it was a stressful situation with Andrew and Abby being so overbearing and controlling.

Lizzie and Emma were prepared to listen to a lecture on the evils of a relationship with a man. Andrew did not disappoint. As soon as he and Abby were seated, he began his rant. Andrew directed his opening to Emma, "I'm sure your sister has already informed you of the stranger she spoke with earlier this morning. I will tell you the same as I said to her. Stay away from that man. We do not need, nor do we want, outsiders in this house. You have everything you need here and you do not need to marry, thus there is no need to speak to any man. I have told you before that having a man in your life will only cause problems in the family. Now leave things as they have always been. Is that understood?" Andrew directed the end of his rant towards Lizzie.

Both girls in unison said, "Yes, Father."

Everyone in the family knew that if either of the girls would defy their father, it would most definitely be Lizzie. Andrew always said Lizzie was exactly like his cousin Eliza, who had been most defiant. He had made it a point to remind his daughters, at least weekly, of the troubles a man had brought to Eliza.

Andrew and Eliza had been close from childhood until she found a suitor. This man pursued Eliza relentlessly. Andrew openly objected, but the family told him that Eliza's affairs were none of his business. Eliza had married this man, much to Andrew's disapproval. Eliza and her husband had two small children, a boy and a girl. It wasn't even a year after the second child, the girl, was born that her husband disappeared. Everyone in town was certain that he had run off; no longer wanting to be tied down.

Eliza was heartbroken. She couldn't believe that her husband would have left her. Jus the night before his disappearance, he had declared his undying love for her and their children. Eliza, having no means to support herself and her children, moved into Andrew's house. Eliza only became more depressed as the days passed. She had only been living with Andrew about three months when she broke.

It was an early spring morning in 1844. A young Andrew Borden awakened to a ghastly discovery. He had gone downstairs to the kitchen to have breakfast with Eliza and her two children. He waited a half an hour but none of them came to join him. He went to Eliza's bedroom fearing she was ill and knocked on the door. There was no answer, so he slowly opened it, calling her name. He was horrified to find that she lay in a pool of blood with a bloody razor still in her hand. She had cut her own wrists and bled to death.

Andrew raced to the children's rooms but they were not there. He searched the rest of the house; still no children.

Andrew made his way to the back yard and still there was no sign of either child. His heart skipped a beat when he noticed the cover to the well was ajar. When he neared the well, he saw the tiny bodies of both children floating in the well. It was apparent that Eliza, stricken with grief by the assumed desertion of her husband, had drowned her own children before committing suicide. Andrew was devastated. He had so loved Eliza—more so than anyone else. He also loved her children as if they were his own.

CHAPTER 3

The days passed and Lizzie could not dispel the thought of the beautiful stranger who was now her neighbor. She so longed to see him again. Just as she had given up hope, the doorbell sounded. Lizzie couldn't imagine who would be calling on the Borden's—so few did.

To Lizzie's surprise, John Goodman stood on the threshold when Bridget answered the door.

"Hello, Mr. Goodman, so nice to see you. I assume you are here to see Mr. Borden?" Bridget said.

"Yes. I wanted to introduce myself. I thought it would be neighborly. I would have the other day when I was by, but had a million things to attend to. My schedule has finally cleared up somewhat and I thought I would pop in for a brief introduction. Is Mr. Borden receiving guests?" John asked.

"I will check. Would you like to come in?" Bridget gestured toward the parlor where Lizzie was sitting.

"Thank you very much," John replied as he took off his hat and handed it to Bridget.

As Bridget hung up his hat and went to find Andrew Borden, John walked into the parlor and greeted Lizzie with a gentle kiss on the back of her hand. Still holding her hand he said, "Ah Lizzie, what a pleasant surprise."

Lizzie smiled and responded, "I do live here. Is it really a surprise that you would find me here in my own home?" She giggled slightly.

Andrew entered the parlor and cleared his throat at seeing the pair. "Huh, hem,"

Lizzie jumped and pulled her hand from John.

"Lizzie," Andrew said while glaring at her.

That's all it took—without hesitation Lizzie left the room

with her head bowed. John was stunned at the strange interaction between Andrew Borden and his lovely daughter.

Andrew asked, "How can I help you, Sir?"

John extended his hand, but Andrew only stood and starred at him. Once again, Andrew asked, "How can I help you?"

John dropped his hand and introduced himself. At receiving no reply, he explained his reason for his visit. "I was taken by your daughter, Lizzie. I know this is very sudden, but I would like to ask your permission to court Lizzie."

Not wanting to draw suspicion and have outsiders speculate about their way of living, Andrew thought it would be best to let Lizzie turn her suitor down herself. He felt certain that she would not go against his wishes. "Well, as you can see, Lizzie is well beyond the age of having to ask her father for permission to court. She is thirty—practically an old maid. Feel free to ask her yourself."

Andrew then called for Lizzie, Who entered the room wondering what Andrew could possibly want from her. "Yes, Father?"

"Well Lizzie, apparently Mr. Goodman is asking for permission to be your suitor. I told him that since you were so old, that he would need ask you for permission."

Lizzie was utterly stunned. She had not expected this inquiry from John and she had definitely not expected this reaction from her father. She knew what her answer should be—the right answer, according to her father. Lizzie only thought for a moment. She knew the repercussions for giving the wrong answer, but she was so taken be John that she didn't care. "Oh my, Mr. Goodman, this is so sudden. I scarcely know you. However, you are a very intriguing man and I am not currently promised to anyone. I would be honored." Lizzie knew, without looking at her father, what expression he wore on his face. She also knew there would be Hell to pay when John left. She surprised herself by her own answer.

"Well then, it's settled. I will make you the happiest woman in the world. You won't regret your decision," John told her, beaming.

Lizzie was already regretting her decision, but she was drawn to John. The moment she met him in the garden she knew she wanted to spend the rest of her life with him, have babies with him, and grow old with him. Lizzie smiled, "I'm sure I won't."

"Thank you, Mr. Borden. I am an honorable man and I will treat your daughter very well." John extended his hand once again, but Andrew did not take it.

Andrew Borden just said, "Umph," and walked away.

John wasn't sure exactly what he had done to offend Andrew Borden and he really didn't care; he had gotten what he had came for—the permission to court Lizzie. "Well Lizzie, I should go now. Could I call upon you tomorrow?"

Lizzie smiled and replied, "That would be delightful. I look

18

forward to it."

John took Lizzie's hand and lightly kissed the back of it. A shiver went up her spine. She looked on longingly as John Goodman retrieved his hat from the hat rack and walked out the front door.

As soon as Emma and Bridget heard the front door open and shut, they came bounding into the parlor where Lizzie sat in disbelief. "Well, tell us everything!" Emma exclaimed as the two girls plunked down on the couch beside Lizzie. "Was he charming? What did Father say? Well, out with it, Lizzie. What's with you? Has the cat got your tongue?" Emma questioned without giving Lizzie a chance to answer.

"I will tell you everything; just give me a minute," Lizzie replied. The three settled in for her to give them the details. But just as she began her story, Andrew walked into the parlor.

Andrew pointed at Emma and Bridget, "You two, leave now!" Then he directed his attention to Lizzie. "What in God's name are you doing? You know the way I feel about men and you becoming involved with one. You very well knew the answer you should have given that man—it surely was not supposed to be *yes!*"

Lizzie was more outgoing and bolder than her sister, even though she had never outright defied her father. Andrew feared that one day Lizzie would become uncontrollable—he had hoped it wouldn't happen.

Lizzie couldn't believe what came from her mouth. "I am thirty years old. You can no longer treat me as a child. A man has finally been brave enough to come here and ask to be my suitor. You left the decision to me and I have made it. I intend to see John and there is nothing you can do to stop me!" Finished, she turned and stomped out of the room.

Andrew was stunned at her actions, though not entirely surprised. He would not let this relationship go anywhere. He was already contemplating a way to stop it. If he had to, he would resort to the same actions he had taken with Eliza. He would make certain Lizzie's suitor would disappear without a trace.

CHAPTER 4

The weeks passed and John and Lizzie saw more and more of one another. Andrew made it obvious to everyone that he was not pleased. He never accepted John's handshake and never spoke to him. He ignored Lizzie in hopes that he could force her to end her ridiculous relationship with John.

One afternoon, John arrived to take Lizzie on a picnic. She took great pains to ensure that everything was perfect—her hair, her clothes and her perfume. She anxiously awaited John's arrival, not unlike any other time John had visited. Lizzie heard the doorknocker and glided from the parlor to the foyer, knowing exactly who was at the door.

Bridget answered the door to find John Goodman standing there, hat in hand. "Good morning, Bridget," he said to the maid. Then he noticed Lizzie standing behind Bridget in the entryway of the parlor. He quickly turned his attention to Lizzie.

"Lizzie," he said, bowing and handing his hat to Bridget. Reaching out he took Lizzie's hand and grazed the back of it with a light kiss. "You look fabulous."

John had been holding one hand behind his back since walking into the house, causing Lizzie's curiosity to grow. "John, what are you holding behind you?"

John brought forth a beautiful silver music box. Lizzie's eyes lit up in delight. Before she could say a word, John opened the box and a song played with such precision and clarity that Lizzie's eyes welled with tears.

"Oh, John, it plays Fur Elise." Lizzie took the box from John and sat down. She had never before been given such a thoughtful gift before and couldn't stop staring at the box while the music played.

John smiled, knowing he made her happy. "Lizzie, I was wondering, before we go out, may I speak to you and your father?"

Lizzie was still mesmerized by her beautiful music box, but she quickly snapped out of it. She couldn't imagine why John would want to speak with her father. "Of course you may. However, I'm not sure if Father will speak to you or I. I have been given the cold shoulder lately," Lizzie replied. "Bridget, would you please fetch Father? And, Bridget, would you please take my music box to my room?"

"Yes, Ms. Lizzie." Bridget took the music box from Lizzie.

"Thank you," Lizzie said.

Bridget bowed out of the room and scurried away to find Andrew Borden.

Lizzie questioned John, "What is so important that you need to speak to me and Father both about?"

"Oh my little impatient Lizzie, you will just have to wait and see," John said with a smile.

"John Goodman, you know I can't stand secrets and I can't

stand to wait a moment on anything. Can't you just tell me now while we are waiting? And what if Father won't come to speak to you? Then will you tell me or must I wait until Hell freezes over?" Lizzie pleaded with John as she tugged at his arm like an impatient child.

John put his hand upon hers, "If Mr. Borden doesn't agree to speak with me, then I will tell you when we settle into our picnic. Will that suit you, Ms. Borden?"

"I prefer to know now, but I guess the picnic will be better than when Hell freezes over," Lizzie said with a giggle.

Andrew stomped into the room forcing Lizzie to quickly wipe the smile from her face and quiet her giggles. John extended his hand to Andrew, which Andrew refused. "What is it?" he said, directing his question to Lizzie.

Lizzie wrung her hands and said to her father, "John needs to speak with you."

Andrew looked at John with cold, hate-filled eyes. "Well?"

"Mr. Borden, I am very fond of your daughter and we have been seeing each other for several months now. I would like to ask your permission to marry Lizzie," John said in anticipation of Andrew's response.

Andrew's faced screwed up in a fashion that Lizzie had never before seen. She was thrilled and surprised by John wanting to marry her. She was also concerned with her father's reaction. The look on Andrew's face let her know that this could not end well.

Andrew knew that he could not deny John's request; Lizzie was neither too young nor was she promised to anyone else. John had a good income and was well bred. Andrew said through his teeth, "Do as you wish, but I curse this relationship." He then stomped from the room, screaming for Abby.

Lizzie knew Abby would be the first to catch the brunt of his anger, then Bridget and Emma. She knew he would save the best for last and that when she returned home there would be

Hell to pay. She didn't care. It would only be a matter of time until she was out from under the control of Andrew and in a safe and loving home with her beloved John.

John was stunned at Andrew's reaction. He knew that Andrew did not care for him at all and that he was a very controlling man, but to see him react in such a way was a shock. He turned to Lizzie, "I am so sorry if I have caused any trouble for your family. I didn't mean to; I only want you to be my wife."

"Oh, John. I am thrilled and I would love to be your wife. Don't worry about Father, nothing makes him happy and everything gets him upset. Now let's go on our picnic and discuss wedding plans," Lizzie said as she grabbed John's hand and the picnic basket.

Andrew had given up his search for Abby and happened by an upstairs window where he noticed Lizzie and John leaving the house. Twisted thoughts and images flooded his mind as he wrung his hands and paced. He would not allow this. One way or another, he would prevent this union.

CHAPTER 5

John arrived one afternoon to take Lizzie for a walk. John had a slight case of the tremors he was still uncomfortable around Andrew even though it had been months since he had asked for Lizzie's hand in marriage and Andrew became angry.

When John knocked on the door, he was surprised when Andrew answered instead of Bridget.

"Hello, Mr. Borden. Is Lizzie home?" John asked.

Andrew didn't say a word; he only gestured to John to come inside. John entered the house looking around for Lizzie, or any sign of the other women who lived there. But no one appeared to be home except Andrew.

Andrew had been waiting to take care of this John Goodman problem and he finally saw his chance. He gestured with his hand for John to enter the parlor. As John walked toward the couch to take a seat Andrew grabbed a huge, silver candelabra and struck John in the head multiple times with all his might.

Poor John never knew what hit him. He sank to the floor, dead from the first blow. That did not stop Andrew from his vengeful abuse upon John, as his repeated blows crushed John's head until he was unrecognizable.

Lizzie and Emma returned home after having gone to the mercantile store to purchase a few supplies. Terrified, Lizzie dropped everything she was holding and ran to John. Even though his face was unrecognizable, she could tell who it was by his shoes, his hat and a ring he wore on his pinky finger—the ring that that was to be Lizzie's wedding band. They had purchased the ring together just a few days earlier.

Emma remained frozen in place as a shriek pierced the air. Andrew ran to Emma and slapped her in the mouth knocking her to the ground, silencing her by the shock of his actions. He quickly slammed the door closed to keep their neighbors from seeing what transpired, then turned to Emma. "You, my good daughter, shall quiet yourself lest you end up like Mr. Goodman," Andrew said as he kicked her in the side.

Emma lay there and wept, fearing that her father would make good on his word.

Andrew turned his attention to Lizzie who knelt beside her fiancé, rocking back and forth quietly sobbing, "Why, Father? Why?" Lizzie was in shock and could barely breathe. As hard as she tried, she could not scream. The room began to spin as Andrew approached her. Her fear took hold of her and she collapsed beside of her beloved John.

Andrew took advantage of this opportunity and quickly dragged John's body to the basement. He drew a hatchet from where it hung on the wall and began to hack the corpse of John into smaller, more manageable pieces. He then dug several holes in the dirt floor of the basement where he buried the remains. He cleaned the blood and mess from the basement and returned upstairs to take of matters there.

Andrew bound into the parlor where Emma cradled Lizzie's head in her lap. With an eerie calm about him that Emma had never before witnessed, he walked over and grabbed her up by the arm. "Where is that no good Maggie?"

Emma said in a quiet trembling voice. "I don't know where Bridget is."

"Has your stepmother not awakened from all the commotion?" Andrew said, squeezing Emma's arm as if to blame her for Abby's laziness.

"I haven't seen her. I-I guess she is still sleeping," Emma stammered.

"Go wake her, now. Tell her to get down here or there will be a heavy price to pay," Andrew said through gritted teeth as he shoved Emma toward to stairs.

Emma stumbled, nearly falling. As soon as she regained her balance, she ran upstairs to retrieve Abby. She ran into the bedroom where Abby was sleeping soundly. It was no wonder that she had not heard the happenings downstairs; she was snoring so loudly that Emma thought not even a train could have jarred her from her slumber. "Stepmother!" she exclaimed as she shook Abby from her sleep.

"What is it? This had better be an urgent matter!" Abby growled at Emma.

"Father needs you right away. He said if you didn't come there would be a hefty price to pay!" Emma spat back.

Abby jumped to attention. "What is it? What is so important?" Abby asked as she round the banisters and began to descend the stairs.

"Father has done something terrible!"

Abby stopped abruptly. "What has he done?"

"It's John—he's dead. Father," Emma became hysterical.

"Oh no! Hush now! Come!" Abby exclaimed as she grabbed Emma by the arm and ushered her forward down the stairs almost pushing her down.

When they reached the parlor, Abby looked around to see blood—lots of blood—and Lizzie lying on the floor next to a pool of crimson with Andrew standing there with his arms crossed. "Andrew, what have you done?" she said before she could stop herself.

"You just don't worry about that. You get Lizzie roused and then the three of you clean up this mess before anyone comes snooping. Everyone knows that Lizzie and John are engaged to be married. It will not be long before he is missed and this is the first place they will be looking for him. Now go, quickly!" Andrew shouted.

Not only had poor Lizzie lost her beloved John at the brutal hands of her father, but she also had to clean up the murder scene. It was almost too much for her to bear. Lizzie was still somewhat in shock and sobbing uncontrollably, but it wasn't long before she became numb as she cleaned away John's blood, brains, and bones from the carpet. The numbness never really left her.

Bridget came home just as the three women were finishing

up. She knew something had happened—something bad by the

tears and actions of Lizzie and Emma, and by the unnatural

nervousness of Abby. Bridget, however, knew not to ask

questions. She knew Lizzie would tell her everything when it

was safe to tell.

"Well, well. It's about time you returned. Where have you

been?" Andrew bounded through the door after having cleaned

himself up.

Bridget lowered her head and responded quietly. "It is my

day off. I went to see my mother."

"Well, no matter. Everything has been taken care of. Are

you making dinner or not?" Andrew said through his teeth as he

glared at Bridget.

"Well, yes I can. Lizzie and Emma usually do on my days off,

but I will."

"See that you do—and now. I am famished," Andrew said as he pointed toward the kitchen.

The three Borden women cleaned themselves up and came back down to eat, even though Lizzie and Emma were sick and could not eat a bite if they wanted to.

The evening meal was eerily silent.

CHAPTER 6

The next day, Lizzie never got out of bed. Emma took her meals to her but didn't touch her food. Fur Elise filled the room as Lizzie just lay there and wept while cradling her music box. She didn't say a word to anyone. Lizzie was totally lost—she just thought about John and the life they could have had.

As Emma was preparing breakfast for Lizzie, she whispered to Bridget, "Father killed John last night."

Bridget dropped the plate she was holding and watched it shatter on the floor. She knew Andrew would lecture her about the cost of the plate and how the cost would be coming out of her pay. Snapping out of her daze, she lowered her voice when she spoke. "Miss Emma, you shouldn't say such things. What if he hears you?"

"It's the truth. I don't know exactly what happened. John

was already dead when Lizzie and I returned home." Emma continued to quietly tell Bridget all that she knew. Bridget was stunned; she knew Andrew was a brutal and cruel man, but she had no idea that he would or could go that far.

The subject was quickly dropped by everyone in the house but was never forgotten. In time, Lizzie gained the ability to deal with her grief, but something had changed in her since John's death. She thought she might be losing her mind when she began to see things.

One night about three weeks after John had been murdered, after the police investigation and after they had determined John had probably met with some ill fate on one of his business trips, Lizzie found herself awakened by her music box playing in the middle of the night. She couldn't understand how that could be. However, she wearily pulled herself from her bed to close the box. The cool floor under her feet roused her a bit more.

Lizzie closed the music box and as the music stopped, she

heard a rustling in the room just behind her. Filled with terror, she slowly turned. Her heart pounded as if she had just ran a mile. Beads of sweat rolled off of her face as if she had just been caught in a downpour and she trembled as if facing her father's wrath.

As Lizzie turned she stammered, "Wh-who's there?" There was no audible response, but when she completed her turn, she was face to face with a woman. This woman was almost transparent. With a trembling hand, Lizzie reached out to touch her, but her hand went right through the woman. Then suddenly the music box began to play again. Lizzie turned and quickly shut it. When she turned back around the woman was gone.

Lizzie jumped back in bed and pulled the covers over her head like frightened child who had just had a nightmare. She lay there all night unable to sleep. Finally, dawn began to shed a little light into her bedroom window. The soft warm glow of the light reassured Lizzie and she was able to fall back to sleep, but only for a short while.

Emma came into the room to see why Lizzie hadn't come down for breakfast. Lizzie was still fast asleep so Emma gently shook her, "Lizzie, Lizzie, wake up. You need to come down for breakfast. Father is getting upset."

Lizzie only stirred enough to say, "I'm not hungry. I am very tired. Please let me rest." And with that, she pulled the covers up over her head and fell back into a deep slumber where she dreamt of her and John.

Emma went back down to the dining room. She tried to explain to her father that she thought Lizzie may be getting sick—why else would she be so tired? Andrew growled the word 'fine' and continued with his breakfast.

When Lizzie awoke, it was to the sound of Fur Elise playing on her music box. She was puzzled and frightened, as she had never heard or seen anything out of the ordinary in their house before. She believed in ghosts, spirits and such, but had never seen one. She was convinced that was what she had seen the night before—a ghost. But who and why, and why had it played her music box?

As the days passed, Lizzie saw more and more of the spectral woman, but no one else mentioned having seen her. The music box played on its own throughout most of the night—every night. Lizzie was so tired during the day that for weeks she barely left her room.

By then, Andrew was beginning to get upset with Lizzie, calling her lazy and willful. One morning he went down to breakfast again to find no Lizzie. Everyone else was at the table knowing that, once again, Andrew was going to make the meal miserable because Lizzie refused to come down and join them.

Andrew looked around before yelling at the top of his lungs, "Lizzie!" With his entire body shaking from anger, he turned and bounded up the stairs. Lizzie was in such a sound sleep, tired from having been up all night, that she didn't hear Andrew yelling. Andrew threw open Lizzie's bedroom door.

Lizzie never stirred. This only infuriated Andrew further. He stomped over to the bed and grabbed her by the arm, jerking her from her bed. She stumbled and could barely stand from exhaustion.

Lizzie was shocked by the rude awakening and her arm throbbed under the excruciating pain of her father's tight grip. "What? What do you want of me? You took what I loved most in the world! Now, just let me lay up here and die from my broken heart. Leave me, or I will make you wish that you had!" Lizzie jerked her arm from Andrew and threw herself backwards into her bed.

Andrew was stunned. Lizzie had been, on occasion, slightly defiant, but never like this. He thought she must be possessed by a demon or a witch. This was not the daughter he knew. He leaned over to be face to face with Lizzie, growling obscenities and spraying her face with spittle. That made Lizzie angrier and the music box slowly opened and Fur Elise began to play. She could take no more.

Lizzie jumped from her bed, pushing Andrew to the floor on his back. She straddled him and began to squeeze his neck with both hands. The warmth of his skin and the sticky sweat that covered him from his wrath under her fingers disgusted her, but she was not going to let go until he was dead. Lizzie heard a whisper in her ear, *"Yes, Dear, that's it. Just a bit more and both you and I will be free of this tyrant. Vengeance for us both, Lizzie."* Lizzie didn't turn to see who was whispering in her ear, but she could tell by the look on Andrew's face as he looked over her shoulder, that he saw the same woman that had taken up residence in Lizzie's room.

Emma and Abby heard the thundering of the scuffle and ran upstairs to break up the argument before it turned violent. They thought they would be protecting Lizzie from Andrew. However, they were surprised by what they saw. They ran to Lizzie, pulling her kicking and screaming from Andrew. "Let me go! He killed John! He deserves to die!"

Andrew rolled over coughing and trying to catch his breath.

Lizzie was fighting to escape the clutches of Emma and Abby, but they held tight until she calmed down. After several minutes when Andrew began to breathe normally, he stood up and walked towards Lizzie. He reared back his hand and slapped her in the face with all his might.

Andrew expected her to cry from the pain he had just inflicted. Instead, Lizzie just looked up at Andrew and smiled. Emma and Abby were stunned, but not as surprised as Andrew. He had always kept control over his family, but something was different. Lizzie not only no longer feared him, but hated him. He had lost total control over her.

He stomped from the room and slammed the door shut behind him. With Andrew gone, Emma and Abby released their hold on Lizzie. Not one word was said As she walked back to her bed and covered up. She was sound asleep before Emma and Abby left the room. They just looked at each other in awe and left the room, allowing the music box to continue playing.

Andrew and Abby no longer had their meals with the girls,

nor did they speak with Lizzie. A few days later, Lizzie came from her room and acted as if her life were exactly the same as it was before she had met John Goodman. Emma, Lizzie and Bridget were as close as ever.

However normal Lizzie appeared to be on the outside, she was every bit as disturbed on the inside. She continued to see the woman and began to converse with her. And the woman continued to play the music box that John had given her. Every time the music box played, Lizzie's anger and hatred for Andrew grew within her like a huge fire burning hot and consuming her soul.

CHAPTER 7

As the months turned into two years, Lizzie's and the music box became inseparable. With the box, also came a constant companion in the form of the woman from her room.

August 4, 1892—The two-year anniversary of John's death, Lizzie woke up to the sound of the mysterious woman whispering in her ear. *"Lizzie, wake up. It's time for Andrew to pay his dues."*

When Lizzie opened her eyes, the music box was playing and the translucent woman was sitting on the edge of her bed. Lizzie had awoken in a state of uncontrollable rage. Fur Elise played so loudly that she knew her eardrums would burst. She leapt from her bed, discounting the woman sitting on the edge. Lizzie went right through her as she arose and slammed the music box shut, but the music continued even louder than before. Lizzie, held her ears but it did not help. She fell to her knees and cried out. Surprised the sound of her voice extinguished the music; Lizzie stood up and looked around for the woman. But the woman was nowhere to be seen.

Lizzie thought the woman spoke to her once again, but when she turned around no one was there. When Lizzie realized the woman's voice was emitting words from within her own mind; the music box opened and began to play softly to soothe Lizzie. She reached over and took the little silver box—the only thing she had left of her beloved John.

Lizzie sat on the edge of the bed as tears flowed freely down her face like a warm salty waterfall. The loss of John flooded her soul. The woman took advantage of this and repeated over and over in Lizzie's head, *"You know what must be done. You know he must pay and so must Abby. Abby is always at his side doing whatever he says. Never objecting to any of his crimes. Now Lizzie! Now!"*

Trance-like Lizzie slowly closed the little music box and put it in her pocket. She went directly down to the basement and retrieved the very hatchet Andrew had used on her sweet John two years earlier. Lizzie then ascended the stairs back into the first floor of their home and climbed the stairs to Abby and Andrew's bedroom where Abby was putting away her freshly laundered dresses.

Lizzie was as quiet as a church mouse as she stood in the doorway of that room. She felt in her pocket to make certain that her music box was still with her. Even though the box was closed, she could have sworn that she heard it playing, taunting her to do what must be done. Without warning, Lizzie thrust the hatchet into Abby over and over. When she finished, a soft, comforting voice soothed Lizzie's throbbing ears with velvet words. *"Ah, Lizzie. Justice, Justice. Now just wait for Andrew; he will be here soon."*

Lizzie sat and waited on the gold settee while the music box played Fur Elise until Andrew arrived. She heard the front door open and shut. She tip-toed to the top of the stairs to catch a glimpse of Andrew and then went back to the settee and sat. There she waited a little longer until he was sleeping. The woman's voice egged her on. *"Now Lizzie. It's time to finish what Andrew began all those years ago. Make him pay for what he did to you—to me."*

Lizzie closed her music box and slipped it back into her pocket, yet she could still hear the song playing. It was haunting. Lizzie slipped down stairs and took care of Andrew with that same hatchet—still covered in Abby's blood. She thrust it into Andrew over and over, though she was certain that the first blow had done him in. She just couldn't stop—the woman would not let her stop. She told Lizzie repeatedly, *"He must pay. He took everything from you—he took everything from me. Don't stop!"*

Lizzie finally stopped swinging the hatchet and leaned over and kissed her father on the forehead. "Now, father, I love you once again. You have paid for your crime."

Bridget came in from the garden. "Oh, Lizzie what have you done?"

Lizzie stood there, blood spattered all over her and the house. She said not a word while holding the blood-drenched hatchet in her hand. Bridget shook Lizzie hard, "Lizzie! Lizzie! Hurry we have to clean you up and get rid of this damned hatchet!"

Lizzie finally snapped back to reality and began to cry. "What have I done? What do I do? They will surly hang me for this!"

"Just do what I say and they will never know it was you. But we must hurry," Bridget assured Lizzie.

Lizzie shook her head in uncertainty still sobbing—not from sadness, but from fear of being caught.

Bridget took Lizzie by the arms and guided her into the kitchen where she quickly stripped and cleaned Lizzie. They burned her clothes in the stove and buried the hatchet in the dirt. Bridget concocted a story about where they were and what they had been doing. She explained that she had been washing windows and did not see or hear anything.

Bridget told Lizzie she should tell the investigators that she was in the garden reading and did not hear or see anything out of the ordinary until she came into the house to find her parents hacked to death.

Lizzie prepared herself complete with hysterics and tears. Bridget stayed at the house with the corpses of the Borden's while Lizzie frantically ran to the neighbors house screaming that someone had killed her parents. Lizzie played the part of the grieving daughter well. The police came and went, taking the corpses with them.

Lizzie and Bridget spent the evening cleaning the aftermath. Lizzie was surprised not to have seen nor heard the spectral woman since the murders. The music box had not played with the help of an unseen hand since the murders either. Her sleep was not interrupted by the translucent woman, however, she had nightmares. She dreamt of the mysterious woman and a man—the woman's husband. She dreamt that a much younger Andrew had used a hatchet to murder and dismember her husband.

Lizzie woke drenched in sweat and trembling as if she had really witnessed that murder. She lay awake until dawn when she finally fell into a deep, restful slumber and did not wake until almost noon—just in time for her sister's return home. She dressed and waited on Emma in the parlor.

Emma returned to find her parents had been murdered. Lizzie confided in Emma about how they really died, leaving her sister in a state of shock, but also with a sense of relief. She could not believe that Lizzie had liberated them from their tyrannical father and neglectful stepmother.

Emma asked Lizzie and Bridget, "What should I tell the police when they question me?"

"Tell them the truth about where you were and when you returned home. Do not say anything else. There is no need to," Lizzie prompted her sister as she held Emma's hand

CHAPTER 8

The police investigation continued and they charged Lizzie

with the murders. In June 1893, Lizzie was tried and acquitted

of the brutal and savage murders of Andrew and Abby Borden.

After the trial, Lizzie, Emma and Bridget decided to pack their

belongings and move to another home in Falls River.

When the girls were in the attic going through boxes, they

found a box of old pictures. In that box they made a hair-raising

discovery. The box held photos of the Borden family. Lizzie

picked up an old worn photo of a woman—the woman Lizzie

had been seeing until the murders when she abruptly stopped

appearing to her.

Lizzie turned the picture over to find the words on the back

were more haunting than the picture itself; *To my loving

Andrew. Always yours, Eliza Borden.*

THE MUSIC BOX MURDERS

53

Ronda L. Caudill grew up in the small rural town in VA and married her high school sweetheart. They have been happily married for 25 years and have two wonderful daughters. Ronda earned her Ph.D. in Education from Capella University. She is the author of Birthright (A Nobleman Novel), The Choice (A Nobleman Novel), Forbidden Fruit, Ravenshire, The Forgotten (The Glass House Children of Ravenshire) and short story A Night at the Bishop House.

www.ingramcontent.com/pod-product-compliance
Lightning Source LLC
Chambersburg PA
CBHW070649130626
46555CB00006B/2781